Let me introduce myself, since its only polite. I'm Jorda nd saved 500 people from death. Yes, that's me, and I'm happy to b : with you. I also hope you're ready for a beautiful adventure witl i- ness, anger, and shock. I'm ready for this and I hope you are toc

"Hey, Hesh, how are you today?" I asked, as I pasted his office.

"It's been hard man... all this damn paperwork. I feel like it's coming from thin air," Hesh said, laughing.

"Well, I'm sorry man, but I get the fun work," I said, smirking at him.

"Listen, if I could be smart like you, I would be helping you," Hesh said.

"So, you guys not doing your work now?" asked Jay, peaking around the conner.

"Wow, you creep... but yeah Hesh is not doing his work," I said, laughing.

"Wow, you ass. Jay, don't listen to him; I am doing my work, don't worry!" Hesh yelled out, so Jay could hear him from the hallway.

I went to my office, looking at what I was working on last. Which was my new suit design. It still had the all black with the red lighting around the suit. I changed the weight of the suit by making it lighter than the TCM1 The Creator Mark 1.

"Cora, show me project TCM2 please."

"Yes, Sir; here is where you left off."

The helmet is a very important part of this suit. Everything in this helmet is important to the rest of the suit. The helmet has the whole suit in it while this little circle has everything in it, including the helmet. It's touch sensitive, along with neural activation for the helmet opening or just wanting the whole suit off in seconds, instead of minutes.

"Cora, does everything match as of now?"

"Some parts won't fully activate around your body yet."

"So, I need to fix the code," I said, walking over to my computer.

"The hologram of the suit shows which parts won't fully activate."

"You want to tackle this together Cora?"

"Sure, Jordan."

Cora and I started to work on the suit for a while, but there were still some problems with it. Honestly, I expected problems; the good thing is we have other problems sorted out.

"Cora what else is not working?"

"Well, when we changed the code for the activation, other parts started to fail."

"Okay, well if you get anything, let me know. I have to see Scarlet for our date."

"Okay, I will let you know, Sir. Have a good rest of your day."

"Thank you, Cora," I said, as I shut my computer down. I made my way down to the bottom of the tower to see Scarlet. She was waiting outside of the front doors, which where glass. "Hey, beautiful, why didn't you come up?"

"Your security didn't let me," she said, laughing.

"Well, you know me; security is number one nowadays," I replied, laughing as well.

"I just didn't want to bother you, so I waited down here is all."

"Well, I'm glad I get to spend the night with you now," I said, smiling.

"Well, Creator, I hope you have good date spots," she said, smiling and giggling.

"Well, this would be my first time, but I think I have a place."

"Oh really, you do?"

"Yeah, I do actually," I said, smiling.

"Where is this spot at?" Scarlet asked, as she started to look around to see if she could guess.

"It's off-world, so no need to look around," I said, laughing.

"Off-world huh? Well, I'll give it to you... I'm interested, Jordan," she said, with an interested face.

I opened a portal to the Peace Planet; I mean, could you blame me? It's an amazing planet where no one can bother us. Also, it's the Peace Planet; the view is extraordinary...the scenery is breathtaking... like, nothing could be better.

"Wow, Jordan, this is amazing. How did you find this place?"

"This is where I found the Draconic Moonstone, so I renamed it the Peace Planet," I said, looking at the view of the forest where the man sat.

"Wow, well I'll give it to you... this is a good first date spot."

"Well thank you, Scarlet; I'm glad you like it."

We both sat down on the edge of the ruins, and just talked for about 3 hours. We mostly talked about what's been new or what plans we had next. One topic I thought was very interesting that she brought up, was what would I be doing if Earth 1 was never destroyed.

"I really don't know... I was going to try and be a scientist or be one who studied the stars." I said, looking up at them.

"Now that you're living in them, how do you feel about that?" Scarlet asked, intrigued to hear my answer.

"I love it... but I also hate it, because of the war and loss."

"Oh yeah, I guess that would get to everyone," Scarlet said, now regretting asking.

"Scarlet, I give you so much credit for being born into this life."

"What do you mean?"

"Being able to hunt people, but not kill them. I know sometimes you have to. Just me being me, I feel like it's getting easier for me to be The Creator. I'm like the beacon of hope for Earth 2, along with Hesh and Jay."

"It's a big responsibility, Jordan, and you've been doing amazingly for being somewhat forced into this life."

We continued to talk for a bit more, then we went back to Earth 2. We said our goodbyes and went home. I got to my front door and opened it to see someone in my kitchen.

"Can I help you?" I asked, scanning the area for things I could use to attack if need be.

"Jordan, is that you?" the man said as he turned around.

"Uncle Vixen y-you're alive," I said, shocked.

"Yeah, it's me, Jordan. When I heard about this and what you created, I needed to see it for myself," Vixen said, smiling.

"It's been a while; lots unfolded man... it really did. The only people I have left are Hesh and Jay."

"The kids that went into the army, right?"

"Yeah them...they made it with me."

"I'm guessing your parents... they uhh..." Vixen said

"Yeah, they didn't make it either," I said, trying not to get emotional

"I'm sorry, Jordan. I know it must have been hard." Vixen said putting his hand on my shoulder

"It's alright; I got over it. I knew I had to focus on my people, more than what unfolded in the past."

"Wise words, Kid." Vixen said to me

"Thanks. Being The Creator kind of does that to you," I said, laughing for a second.

"I bet it does, kid Well, hey, I'll let you get some rest. I bet it was a long day." Vixen said to me happily

"Thanks, I'll hopefully see you tomorrow." I said stopping him before he left

"Okay, just let me know, Man," I said, hugging him back

"I will," Vixen replied, smiling before leaving.

After Vixen left, I went to take my suit off. The next day, I woke up, went to take a shower, then did everything else someone does when they get up. Putting my suit on is really annoying when getting out of the shower; it really is. Having all the hot air in the suit makes everything humid, so I can't put my helmet on until I'm completely dry. Otherwise, my HUD will be foggy, and I can't see anything. I walked into my office to see Cora working on the suit.

"Good morning, Cora. I see you're working on the suit still," I said, cheerfully

"Yes, I've been up all night and every time I fix something, more problems arise," Cora said, a bit frustrated

"Hey, I'm here now, so let's do this together and I'm sure we will fix it," I said, with confidence. We both sat down and started to work on the suit

"Look at this Cora," I said, as I gestured her to come over to the hologram

"What did you find, Sir?" Cora said interested in what I found

"The chip that activates everything is getting confused. I coded it to open everything at once, so it's trying, but the code is always changing when we update or fix it," I said, trying to see if Cora understands

"So, we need the parts to be opened individually and not all at once?" Cora said looking at the hologram

"Exactly. So, we just have to have them open all at the same time, but individually, so it looks like it's all opening at once," I said, feeling so badass

"Let's try it, Sir." Cora said phasing over to the computer

"Okay, I'll fix it right now and I'll tell you when to activate it." My brain started to fire up with fixing the code, and I added a few new things to the suit, which hopefully you'll find out soon. Fixing the code took around 20 minutes, but it will hopefully be worth it. "Okay, Cora, get ready to open it......now!"

"Okay, Sir." The suit opened like I envisioned it to, and damn it looked beautiful. The metallic black shining in the light of the morning sun. Along with the red LEDs on the helmet, chest, back, legs, and fingers. These LED's made it seem like there were many of them, but there were only four on the chest, two on the helmet, three on two fingers on both hands, five on the back, and two on each leg.

"Isn't she beautiful, Cora? TCM2 is my new baby," I said, with a tear in my eye

"This is an amazing start and discovery for our technology, Sir." Cora said amazed

"Look at that... we made history once again, plus a new start for future suits for others. Honestly, if we keep going with this, people would be able to create clothing, or small weapons to defend themselves," I said, as my mind was gathering new ideas every second

"Let's focus on what we have now, Sir. No need to think of the future just yet," Cora said, laughing

“You’re right, Cora, not yet,” I said, laughing as well After that breakthrough I went to see the boys in the cafeteria. We went to go get their suits made as well, since everything was working; but hopefully, we won’t need to use them for war.

“Congrats on your suit, Man,” Hesh said amazed

“Yeah, I’m very impressed with how you made that work,” Jay said hinting at wanting to see it

“Thanks, Guys, it really means a lot,” I said to them both

“So, what’s next on your mind? Anything new you’re going to build?” Jay asked, curiously

“Umm... I have some things on my mind, but it’s way too early for the idea to be put into play,” I said, thinking about the idea in my head

“That big huh? Well, now I’m really curious,” Jay says, laughing.

“Bro, what could be bigger than the suit you just made?” Hesh said, laughing

“Trust me, the day will come sooner or later, and you’ll see it,” I said, laughing

We all walked to my office and I showed them the suit activating and deactivating.

“Damn, Dude, that’s literally the coolest thing ever. How did you manage to create this?” Hesh asked surprised

“By coding parts to move when they get the signal. It sounds easy but it’s very, very difficult, I must say,” Cora said to Hesh

“What’s the metal used for in the suit?” Jay asked me

“It’s made of Jascyx, a very light metal, but not too strong against heavy attacks,” I explained to them

“Why pick terrible durability?” Hesh says, confused

“Because, if you’re fast, then you won’t get hit. for example, I have been trained to take hits even with my power. So now, I can move faster and fight faster, instead of being slow and taking hits over and over, which will wear me down and cause faster exhaustion for a normal person,” I explained, more in depth

“Okay, but what if they are not fast like you or us?” Jay asked

“I’m not going to force people to wear the new suits I give them; it’s not right, if they are not comfortable with it,” I said to Jay

“All right, well, like I said, the suit is super cool looking,” Jay said We all continued to talked about everything and what would occur if another war happens. Honestly, I’m scared, but also prepared for any future attacks.

Chapter 2
The Unknowns of Space

Space: it's a very complicated thing, super unknown which makes it scarier. My theories of space are still unproven. My questions about space are still unanswered which scares me, but also intrigues me. The only thing I know is that there is life out there; some good and lots of evil. Right now, we are dealing with Space pirates trying to take stuff from Earth 2. My bright mind decided it was a good idea to talk to them.

"Guys and girls, what are you doing to my stuff?" I yelled to them.

"Who are you?" They asked, pulling their swords out

"I'm uhh... The Crea...you really don't know who I am?" I asked, scratching my helmet like I was scratching my head

"No, we don't. So maybe you should walk your ass back that way," they laughed, and continued to take stuff

"Hey umm... I really can't let you take that or you'll have a bad day, so let's put the stuff back," I said, walking towards them

"You really want to die, don't you bitch?" The one big guy said

"Umm I think I should be saying that...not you," I said, dickish.

The big guy walked up to me, trying to be intimidating. He took his sword and rested it on his shoulder, still holding it. "Walk away tiny man. Right now," he said aggressively "Man, you really are taking my lines, aren't you?".

The guy swung his sword at my head and I ducked out of the way. I punched his leg really hard, to make him drop to one knee; when he did, I jumped up and kneed him in the jaw knocking him out.

"Soooo...next?"

Two of them ran toward me, and I dodged the right guy's attack, while grabbing the wrist of the left guy. He dropped his sword and I kicked it away. I pushed the left guy into some boxes. The right guy swung his sword every which way, and honestly, I felt badly because he looked like me fighting with a stick from my backyard. I ducked his one attack, and punched his arm with the sword in it. He dropped it and I kicked him into the wall knocking him out. The left guy now got his sword and tried to cut me in the back, but I grabbed the blade of the sword and snapped it in half. Kicking his legs out from under him, he started to look scared of me.

"Yes, we will leave and put everything back," they said, very nervously.

"Thank you; have a nice day. Also, I'll have people watching you, to make sure you put everything back, along with a search of your Space Curser or ship... that's confusing." I walked away from them and went to The Tower to start my day the right way.

Everyone saw me walking in and had a lot to say when I entered. "Just send everything to my office, please; I'm very busy today." I finally got to my office, and, as I opened the door, I saw Hesh and Jay.

"Well, Good morning, Jordan. You wanna tell us why you're on the news?" Hesh said.

"When am I not on the news?" I laughed.

"Well, it says you beat some pirates up on the way to work," Jay said.

"Yeah, I did; what's the problem with that? I said, confused.

"You fought pirates and didn't even ask us to help," Hesh said.

"You're serious right now? You guys are pissed over that?" I asked, a bit annoyed.

"Yes, we are," Jay said.

"What the hell did you want me to do? Call you and twenty minutes later you guys show up, and then they're gone?" I said, pissed.

"Well, it wouldn't be like that; it's more like 9 minutes," Hesh said, screwing with me.

"Get the fuck out. Now."

"Wow, who pissed in your coffee this morning?" Jay said.

"Yeah, really, who did?" Hesh said.

"Now," I said, pissed off.

They walked out of my office and, as they did, I sat in my chair and looked out the window.

"I heard what happened," Cora said, popping out of nowhere.

I jumped, "God damn, you scared me."

"The pirates also got scared because of what happened" Cora said, concerned.

"Well, people shouldn't be able to get away with stuff like that. Also, with Hesh and Jay I just couldn't handle their jokes about something so serious," I said, trying to calm down.

"Jordan, I know I'm an AI, but I understand, okay? Pirates tried to take your stuff and they almost got away with it, but are you going to get mad at that? Nothing is perfect, Jordan; sometimes things happen, even to the best of us. Also, be nicer to your friends; they are here for a reason," Cora said, as she then turned into nothing.

Me being me, I just started to work more. I tried my best to let everything go, but I couldn't. How would you feel if you worked so hard to make something, and someone started to take from it? I'm sure you'd be pissed and upset; now you understand how I feel. So, I got to work on something that would make sure no one could steal my stuff ever again. Well, it's been created before, but hopefully mine is better. They are called cameras. Yes, I know what you're thinking: why didn't have them installed the day we got here? Well, I'll tell you. The reason is because of privacy, you know? Do you like being spied on when you're just doing your daily routine? Probably not. Now, I need them, so I can see people coming; that way, I can be more prepared.

Hesh and Jay walk into my office. "Jordan, are you sure you want to do this?" Jay asked.

"Yes; we will be better prepared, Guys. I don't like the idea either, but we need them," I said, looking at the work.

"There has to be a better way, Jordan... surely," Hesh told me, firmly.

"Well, there isn't, Hesh; I'm sorry, but it needs to be like this," I said, very determined.

"Jordan, don't or we will have a problem," Jay said, getting up out of his chair, along with Hesh doing the same.

"So, this is how we are going to do things then? Looks like you guys just picked a fight you won't win," I stood up and activated my helmet. "Let's dance, Bitches."

Hesh jumped over my desk, and, when he landed, he started to throw punches; I dodged them and kicked his chest, making him fly back. Hesh waited for me to move to him and so I did. I jumped over my desk and did a roll; when I did, I went under Hesh's legs and kicked his back, making him go forward into my desk. Jay got up and starting running toward me. He began to fight in a different style, which I've seen before, but Jay was not too familiar with the style yet, I could tell. Jay did a kick, followed with a punch to the stomach. I fell backward into the hallway. I balled my fist and used it to get up; when I did, I waited for Jay to walk out the doorway. When Jay did, I grabbed him by the neck and threw him out the hallway window.

"No! Jay!" Hesh Screamed.

"Your turn," I said, with a straight face.

"You son of a bitch, you're going to die," Hesh said, enraged.

He tackled me to the ground, and, as he did, he was punching my helmet. I was able to use my knee to kick his back, which was just enough to make him fly forward a bit, I had to get up to knock him out with a big blow to the head.

"Maybe think before you take on someone better than you, Hesh," I said, as I walked away from everything.

As I was walking home, I realized that I didn't care if Jay lived or not. There was no remorse when I threw him out the window. I never knew what happened to them I don't know if they lived or died. Being thrown out of a 2,540-foot tower would kill anyone; for me, I'm sure my bones would just look like pebbles. As I got to my front door, I saw a note in the metal mail slot; it was from Hesh. I pulled the note out from the slit in the door and walked inside to the table. I opened the letter and it read: Jordan, I think it's time we find our own spot in the universe, which I'm sure you saw coming. Being by your side is great

Me being me, I just started to work more. I tried my best to let everything go, but I couldn't. How would you feel if you worked so hard to make something, and someone started to take from it? I'm sure you'd be pissed and upset; now you understand how I feel. So, I got to work on something that would make sure no one could steal my stuff ever again. Well, it's been created before, but hopefully mine is better. They are called cameras. Yes, I know what you're thinking: why didn't have them installed the day we got here? Well, I'll tell you. The reason is because of privacy, you know? Do you like being spied on when you're just doing your daily routine? Probably not. Now, I need them, so I can see people coming; that way, I can be more prepared.

Hesh and Jay walk into my office. "Jordan, are you sure you want to do this?" Jay asked.

"Yes; we will be better prepared, Guys. I don't like the idea either, but we need them," I said, looking at the work.

"There has to be a better way, Jordan... surely," Hesh told me, firmly.

"Well, there isn't, Hesh; I'm sorry, but it needs to be like this," I said, very determined.

"Jordan, don't or we will have a problem," Jay said, getting up out of his chair, along with Hesh doing the same.

"So, this is how we are going to do things then? Looks like you guys just picked a fight you won't win," I stood up and activated my helmet. "Let's dance, Bitches."

Hesh jumped over my desk, and, when he landed, he started to throw punches; I dodged them and kicked his chest, making him fly back. Hesh waited for me to move to him and so I did. I jumped over my desk and did a roll; when I did, I went under Hesh's legs and kicked his back, making him go forward into my desk. Jay got up and starting running toward me. He began to fight in a different style, which I've seen before, but Jay was not too familiar with the style yet, I could tell. Jay did a kick, followed with a punch to the stomach. I fell backward into the hallway. I balled my fist and used it to get up; when I did, I waited for Jay to walk out the doorway. When Jay did, I grabbed him by the neck and threw him out the hallway window.

"No! Jay!" Hesh Screamed.

"Your turn," I said, with a straight face.

"You son of a bitch, you're going to die," Hesh said, enraged.

He tackled me to the ground, and, as he did, he was punching my helmet. I was able to use my knee to kick his back, which was just enough to make him fly forward a bit, I had to get up to knock him out with a big blow to the head.

"Maybe think before you take on someone better than you, Hesh," I said, as I walked away from everything.

As I was walking home, I realized that I didn't care if Jay lived or not. There was no remorse when I threw him out the window. I never knew what happened to them I don't know if they lived or died. Being thrown out of a 2,540-foot tower would kill anyone; for me, I'm sure my bones would just look like pebbles. As I got to my front door, I saw a note in the metal mail slot; it was from Hesh. I pulled the note out from the slit in the door and walked inside to the table. I opened the letter and it read: Jordan, I think it's time we find our own spot in the universe, which I'm sure you saw coming. Being by your side is great

“Yes, we will leave and put everything back,” they said, very nervously.

“Thank you; have a nice day. Also, I’ll have people watching you, to make sure you put everything back, along with a search of your Space Curser or ship... that’s confusing.” I walked away from them and went to The Tower to start my day the right way.

Everyone saw me walking in and had a lot to say when I entered. “Just send everything to my office, please; I’m very busy today.” I finally got to my office, and, as I opened the door, I saw Hesh and Jay.

“Well, Good morning, Jordan. You wanna tell us why you’re on the news?” Hesh said.

“When am I not on the news?” I laughed.

“Well, it says you beat some pirates up on the way to work,” Jay said.

“Yeah, I did; what’s the problem with that? I said, confused.

“You fought pirates and didn’t even ask us to help,” Hesh said.

“You’re serious right now? You guys are pissed over that?” I asked, a bit annoyed.

“Yes, we are,” Jay said.

“What the hell did you want me to do? Call you and twenty minutes later you guys show up, and then they’re gone?” I said, pissed.

“Well, it wouldn’t be like that; it’s more like 9 minutes,” Hesh said, screwing with me.

“Get the fuck out. Now.”

“Wow, who pissed in your coffee this morning?” Jay said.

“Yeah, really, who did?” Hesh said.

“Now,” I said, pissed off.

They walked out of my office and, as they did, I sat in my chair and looked out the window.

“I heard what happened,” Cora said, popping out of nowhere.

I jumped, “God damn, you scared me.”

“The pirates also got scared because of what happened” Cora said, concerned.

“Well, people shouldn’t be able to get away with stuff like that. Also, with Hesh and Jay I just couldn’t handle their jokes about something so serious,” I said, trying to calm down.

“Jordan, I know I’m an AI, but I understand, okay? Pirates tried to take your stuff and they almost got away with it, but are you going to get mad at that? Nothing is perfect, Jordan; sometimes things happen, even to the best of us. Also, be nicer to your friends; they are here for a reason,” Cora said, as she then turned into nothing.

and all, but Jay and I want to do more than paperwork and fight with you. We are friends, not enemies. I'm sorry, Jordan, but this is the right decision, whether you like it or not.

From,

Hesh and Jay

I dropped the note on the table and started to tear up from what I did to my friends. They didn't deserve what I did to them over God damn cameras. I punched the table and it broke. Two legs came off and there was a big hole in it. After all that, I just went to bed, hoping I would forget about everything tomorrow. That's not what happened at all; I ended up staying awake all night, just overthinking about everything, which is not good for anyone. So, I went to my office, sat in my chair, and drank coffee as I watched out my window.

"Jordan, what are you doing here so late?" Cora said as she was forming from mid-air.

"Just thinking I guess, or crying...both works," I said, looking down at my coffee.

"I don't wanna be rude, but you look like shit, Jordan."

"I feel like it more than I look like it," I said, lifting my head up, looking out the window.

"You know looking out the window won't help you, right?" Cora said, walking over to me.

"I know, but Cora, sometimes I wish I died on Earth 1 with everyone else, so I could be with my mother," I said, as I burst into tears.

"Jordan, you need to pull yourself together. I know your friends are gone, but you have millions of people who need you more than ever," Cora said, trying to make me feel better.

"Cora, I don't know if I can; I'm a mess," I said, getting up.

"Take it easy then, Jordan; but you will have to be there for them if something happens."

"Yeah, I'll try my best, Cora. I really will try by using the rest of my energy to either fight, or just except defeat," I said, walking out of my office.

Chapter 3
Total control

The morning came I heard explosions and screaming coming from the city. I put activated my suit and ran out my front door. What I was met with was fire, destruction, and slaughter. I ran into the town which was 16 feet away from my house I saw men in glassy black volcanic rock armor killing my people with swords made of hardened T10 tool steel. This guy and me locked eyes we both ran towards each other. I rolled a bit to the side of him at the same time tripping him. I kicked his sword away from his reach. The guys start to attack but I was able to block most of his attacks but he did get me a couple times on my left rib cage. As the guys threw a punch to my left rib cage again, I let him hit me but lowered my arm to catch his arm and lock it there. I was able to dislocate his arm and punch his helmet to break it into pieces. I swept my leg under his to make him fall again when he did, I snapped his neck killing him instantly. My chest was hurt I was panting from fighting already I was not in good shape to fight at all.

"The Creator...am I right" a voice said 3 feet behind me

"Your damn right" I said breathing heavily

"You have a mask on to I see"

"More like a helmet but whatever you say".

The guy was wearing the same glassy volcanic armor but it was glowing a reddish orange color like lava.

"Trust me Creator I have waited awhile for this...I'm going to love every moment of it" he said with a grin on his face

"I guess we will find out now wont we lava man"

"The name is Vulcan like the Roman religion, God of fire, particularly in its destructive aspects as volcanoes or conflagrations"

"Oh my god you really just had to explain your name to the smartest being in the universe".

Vulcan ran toward me when he got close, he swung his sword. Vulcan was able to strike me it made me tumble back a bit and grab my arm.

and all, but Jay and I want to do more than paperwork and fight with you. We are friends, not enemies. I'm sorry, Jordan, but this is the right decision, whether you like it or not.

From,

Hesh and Jay

I dropped the note on the table and started to tear up from what I did to my friends. They didn't deserve what I did to them over God damn cameras. I punched the table and it broke. Two legs came off and there was a big hole in it. After all that, I just went to bed, hoping I would forget about everything tomorrow. That's not what happened at all; I ended up staying awake all night, just overthinking about everything, which is not good for anyone. So, I went to my office, sat in my chair, and drank coffee as I watched out my window.

"Jordan, what are you doing here so late?" Cora said as she was forming from mid-air.

"Just thinking I guess, or crying...both works," I said, looking down at my coffee.

"I don't wanna be rude, but you look like shit, Jordan."

"I feel like it more than I look like it," I said, lifting my head up, looking out the window.

"You know looking out the window won't help you, right?" Cora said, walking over to me.

"I know, but Cora, sometimes I wish I died on Earth 1 with everyone else, so I could be with my mother," I said, as I burst into tears.

"Jordan, you need to pull yourself together. I know your friends are gone, but you have millions of people who need you more than ever," Cora said, trying to make me feel better.

"Cora, I don't know if I can; I'm a mess," I said, getting up.

"Take it easy then, Jordan; but you will have to be there for them if something happens."

"Yeah, I'll try my best, Cora. I really will try by using the rest of my energy to either fight, or just except defeat," I said, walking out of my office.

Chapter 3
Total control

The morning came I heard explosions and screaming coming from the city. I put activated my suit and ran out my front door. What I was met with was fire, destruction, and slaughter. I ran into the town which was 16 feet away from my house I saw men in glassy black volcanic rock armor killing my people with swords made of hardened T10 tool steel. This guy and me locked eyes we both ran towards each other. I rolled a bit to the side of him at the same time tripping him. I kicked his sword away from his reach. The guys start to attack but I was able to block most of his attacks but he did get me a couple times on my left rib cage. As the guys threw a punch to my left rib cage again, I let him hit me but lowered my arm to catch his arm and lock it there. I was able to dislocate his arm and punch his helmet to break it into pieces. I swept my leg under his to make him fall again when he did, I snapped his neck killing him instantly. My chest was hurt I was panting from fighting already I was not in good shape to fight at all.

"The Creator...am I right" a voice said 3 feet behind me

"Your damn right" I said breathing heavily

"You have a mask on to I see"

"More like a helmet but whatever you say".

The guy was wearing the same glassy volcanic armor but it was glowing a reddish orange color like lava.

"Trust me Creator I have waited awhile for this...I'm going to love every moment of it" he said with a grin on his face

"I guess we will find out now wont we lava man"

"The name is Vulcan like the Roman religion, God of fire, particularly in its destructive aspects as volcanoes or conflagrations"

"Oh my god you really just had to explain your name to the smartest being in the universe".

Vulcan ran toward me when he got close, he swung his sword. Vulcan was able to strike me it made me tumble back a bit and grab my arm.

I walked back up to him I stared at him and went into a kick to the chest when I landed, I struck him in the ribs from the right side. Vulcan dropped to his one knee also looking up at me he didn't seem defeated but almost ready for another round.

"Stay down I don't want to kill you" I said hoping I didn't have to kill him

"You don't get it Creator ...this creation of yours was meant to be taken away from you...your gift to these people was meant to crumble...if you opened your eyes for once maybe you would have seen that sooner" Vulcan said breathing heavy

"My sight is clear is day...your vision is the one clouded with rage and murder. This planet will never be yours Vulcan no matter what you throw at us or at me even. I will always be victorious and you on the other hand will exhale regret and breathe failure".

After saying what needed to be said to Vulcan, I was stabbed with three swords from behind. The swords pierced me through the chest making me fall face first onto the ground. I tried to pick myself up but as I lifted my head Vulcan stepped on my head to walk over me. Vulcan, then kneed down and looked at me. I could tell behind his mask he was grinning and smiling. A lot was going through my head at this point my main thought was where is my friends. "Looks like you lost...Creator" he said giggling

That moment of not being able to breathe at all since my helmet was on. It was scary I was basically suffocating in my own creation which was terrifying to think about as well. I felt hopeless a feeling that I thought I'd never feel again in my life. Accepting death was something I'd never thought I'd have to do either. Even though I can't die I really wanted to in this moment. I couldn't move to open my helmet so I couldn't even get cold air on my face. Scarlet eventually found me lying there basically dead. She really didn't know how to react to me laying there not moving because of the sight of three swords in me.

"Oh my god Jordan are... please tell me your...alive" Scarlet said then started to cry

"S...S...Sca...Scarlet" I said barley able to speak followed with very small inhales

"Jordan, please get up we have to take you somewhere" Scarlet said as she cried more

"Ch...C...Chapel" I said in a whisper

Scarlet, took the swords out of my back so I could start healing properly. Scarlet, then took me to her ship and took me to chapel so he could help me. The journey there was around 50 million light years away let me tell you it felt longer than it should have been. Eventually we got to the monastery where Chapel lives and teaches. Scarlet picked me up slowly while Chapel was walking up to the ship.

"Scarlet, what happened to him" Chapel said very concerned

"He was fighting someone called Vulcan...Jordan was stabbed in the back by three swords and they went through the other side of him" Scarlet said tearing up

"don't worry Scarlet he's safe now I will do everything I can to make sure he's okay...I promise" Chapel said smiling at Scarlet.

Chapel started leading scarlet to the medical chambers. Scarlet, put me on one of the beds slowly making sure my head didn't hit the bed hard. She opened my mask with the button on the side feeling the cold air hit my face felt so good and refreshing. What was followed by my mask opening was tones of half dried blood going all over the brick floor. The smell of old blood filled the little room we were in.

"You scared me Jordan" Scarlet said while tearing up

"I'm sorry Scarlet...I thought I had him...I really thought I did…I lost. Honestly, for a minute I thought I was dead. Just lying there hopelessly really made me feel dead" I said tearing up

"Jordan, I know you tried your best okay but how did you get stabbed"

"Three guys where behind me and stabbed me super quick so I couldn't recover in time…Vulcan was a distraction so they could injure me" I said tearing up from replaying the memory in my head

"Well kid I'm glad you were able to survive" said Chapel walking into the room

"Chapel it's good to see you again...thank you for saving me as well" I said as I sat up

"I'm glad you're not dead kid you really should be more aware of your surroundings and not be cocky like I taught you" he said speaking calmly

"Yeah, I was being cocky you are right" I said with a cough

"Well of course you were kid look at your body…you were too confident with the fight. You see it as having power unlike others that have skill but others may have power just not showing it in till the time comes… that's what through you off your focus. You knew you could beat him but you didn't take one second to think he may have power like you and me" Chapel said wisely

"Yeah, I thought I could he seemed weak and not a lot of training…in till the last second, he wasn't even trying to fight me I was already exhausted from fighting his men" I said replaying the fight in my head

"Chapel, I screwed up...Earth 2 is overrun by a god-awful person. I can't do anything to stop him nor get my Earth back…I'm literally broken" I said with tears rolling down my face like rain droplets

"Jordan, do you really think your broken" Chapel said pointing at me

"Yes, I really do think I'm broken" I said trying to sit up

"Your mind is broken your body is healing now it's up to you to fight and build your mind back up. Pick those broken pieces up and throw them away because you'll be growing a stronger mindset stronger than your last. You're a broken man yes that's because you lost at your own game...on your own creation. So, what are you going to do to get it back sit here and cry and be mad or are you going to become better push your limits to a level that's never been reached before" chapel said in a firm tone

"Yes, I'm going to push myself your damn right I'm going to push myself…people believed in me to protect them I still am going to no matter the fucking cost".

The next day Chapel was training me like his master of old taught him. It was a very unique fighting style that only few know and can master fully. These skills will push you to do things you never wanted to do along with your body being sore for what felt like eternity but over time it became normal. Every shower I took was on the top of the cold mountain with freezing cold icy water. Chapel was beating me with a piece of bamboo if I failed a test to add to that the only type of clothes, I had on was a robe a white and red robe. Nothing was protecting me from the bamboo but every time I'd get hit it would fuel me to do better and think smarter. Sword fighting became easier hand to hand combat became easier I just kept failing at examining my surroundings.

"Come on get up kid" Chapel said

"DAMN IT" I screamed when I fell to the ground after being hit with the bamboo

"Kid get the hell up you're not done" Chapel yelled

"I can't do this anymore I'm hurting everywhere" I screamed at Chapel

"Really, do you think your enemy is going to let you have a break…HELL NO…NOW GET THE HELL UP" Chapel said screaming back at me

Trying to lift my body up off the ground hurt like a bitch but I didn't let that stop me. I ran toward Chapel with my bamboo sword slashing like he taught me to. Up, down low, right side, turn around while ducking, kick legs, jump up, and slash. Chapel still knocked me down which hurt like a bitch once again.

"You've gotten better kid but you still need some work just yet…let your body heal for the rest of the night and we will pick up where we left off tomorrow" Chapel said as he walked away into his house

"Yep, alright see you tomorrow I guess" I said to no one

I got up slowly using my bamboo sword as a helping hand eventually I got up when I did, I went to a little overlook where you can see the villages lights also you can see the stars super clearly. When I was up there, I was just thinking about life and how far I've come also what if I lose everything obviously everyone overthinks about stuff.

"Mom if you can hear me, I just want to say I'm sorry for everything. I lost…it's been hard as you can tell if you were watching me" I said to the stars

"So, what are you doing up here babe" Scarlet said walking up

"Just talking to my mom...if she was listening" I said with a laugh

"I'm sure she's listening to you…somewhere in the universe" Scarlet said smiling

"I hope she isn't upset at me for losing and almost quitting" I said as I looked back up to the stars for a couple seconds

"Jordan, she would understand you almost died. I'm sure if someone lived what you just went through, they wouldn't want to try again" scarlet said hugging me

"Even though I have these powers I feel so powerless" I said looking at my hands while I rubbed them together

"Wow Jordan, that was very deep even for me and I don't have powers…Be glad you do have those powers because you have the ability to try again" scarlet said tearing up

"You always have a place here…I'm sure Chapel would have you be a teacher"

"But that's not what I'm meant to be…I'm meant to be a leader who shows others that even beaten down you can always find the strength to get back up no matter how hard the fight is or how unfair it is. I'm meant to show them that so if I don't, I'll look weak but if I lose all that's gone, I wouldn't be able to live with myself" I said to Scarlet

"I know you'll win you've done so much training more to come you've done more than I have in my first week of being here. Also, you have powers and yet you're still failing and getting hurt. You don't stay down either you get back up every time you are literally making the students motivated to be just like you. So yes, I believe you'll win babe" Scarlet said to me

"I guess your right babe I can do this...It just takes time is all" I gave Scarlet a kiss

"Well, if you want to stay here you can but I'm going to bed"

"Okay babe and yeah, I'm going to stay here" I smiled

"Okay babe I love you" scarlet said

"I love you to"

After Scarlet left, I sat down on the ground still looking up to the stars. I ended up falling asleep in that spot because of how relaxing and quiet it was.

"I see you feel asleep here" Chapel said

"Huh...yeah...yeah, I did" I said rubbing my eyes

"Come on kid training time"

We started to walk down the path to the monastery. When we did, I saw Hesh and Jay standing in the middle training area.

"Hesh...Jay...you guys are here...how? Why?" I said excited

"Scarlet reached out to us about what happened so we thought we'd see our best friend" Jay said

"Yeah, we put all of what happened behind us...we are friends we should be here for each other no matter what happens" Hesh said smiling

I ran to them and hugged them both so tight.

"I'm so sorry guys I spent so many nights wishing I could have taken that all back" I said to them both

"I know man we both are also sorry for all that it was over camera's the dumbest thing to fight over" Hesh said

"So, what's the plan Jordan" Jay said smiling

“Well, I’m training so after I’m fully done with training, we will figure everything out” I said

“Well let’s get to training a bit then guys I’m a bit rusty but I’m sure I still got it” Hesh said stretching

“Yeah, you two idiots are going to get killed” Chapel said

Chapel and I started training I was focusing on the other students more than chapel since I was mainly focused on Chapel and what he was going to do than what the students were going to do. The students started to attack I tripped one blocked attack with my sword. I was able to fake kill the one but the others were still coming. Two came after me while two were behind me waiting to find a weakness. The two guys in front of me ran toward me but I flipped over them now facing all five. I successfully beat the four guys then I faced Chapel I felt so ready to take him on. I ran toward him doing a different combo this time to throw him off which worked. I threw my sword at Chapel and while he was dodging that I swept his feet out from under him. Before he hit the ground, I caught him by his robe and pulled him up.

“Well done kid I’m so proud of you...I’m truly proud of you” Chapel said hugging me tight

“Thank you master Chapel I’m honored to be one of your students” I said while still hugging Chapel

“Kid it was an honor teaching you...I’m proud to say you have completed your training now it’s up to you kid to take back what’s yours” Chapel said

“Yes, I will Chapel don’t worry I won’t fail you...I promise”

Scarlet and I went to the where Hesh and Jay were staying which was very terrible but good, I guess you could say. The house was very nice for a 3-bedroom house the inside was where everything looked better and more modern.

“So, this is our place guys” Hesh said happily

“it’s very nice guys the gray wood flooring and the white walls are nice” I said to them

“Well, the upstairs is a dark oak wood floor with light gray walls so it kind of gets better” Jay said

“Oh, and there is a hot tube plus a pool so enjoy yourselves…oh also you can pick any room upstairs we sleep down here” Hesh said

“Huh you guys…sleep together” scarlet said hoping they don’t say yes

“What no I sleep in the bedroom and Hesh sleeps on the couch” Jay said

“Oh...oh my bad guys” Scarlet said

“But please make yourselves at home” Hesh said

Scarlet and I walked up to our room we picked we started to talk.

“Sorry about earlier I didn’t mean to be like that” I said to scarlet

“What you being all overthinky...yeah, I know your sorry” Scarlet said

"I figured you knew what I was going to say" I said looking at my feet

"Jordan, you say sorry every 4 seconds...I know you really are sorry but being like that is normal for everyone" Scarlet said to me

"I know its normal Scarlet but I shouldn't overthink I should just...think" I said having an idea

"It looks like you have something on your mind" Scarlet said looking at me

"I do have an idea...everyone overthinks you said that mean Vulcan was doing the same either before fighting or during it...or both. Vulcan, has got to be human right?" I blurted out to Scarlet

"Vulcan seemed human and acted like a human would so yeah, I'd say a good 90%" Scarlet said

I told Scarlet to drop me off on the Peace planet so I could do real thinking. Also do some meditation to calm my mind and relax me. Someone from the planet stumbled upon me while I was meditating but he seemed lost maybe hurt not physically but mentally.

"Hey, kid you okay" I said to him

"Wow umm yeah I'm fine" he said shocked to see someone

"No, you're not kid I can see it all over you" I said to him

"that's noticeable" the kid said

"Very…now what's going on I know that there are no villages close to here so why walk this far" I said concerned

"Just needed a break from everyone and everything" the kid said

"Listen I get it I really do...I lost my world to someone terrible he took everything from me at the time humiliated me in front of trillions" I said looking down remembering when I was stabbed

"What so why are you here then" the kid said

"The same thing you're doing here kid...getting away from everything" I said to the kid

"So, what happened when you lost" the kid said taking a seat on the stone slab where my helmet was

"Well, I was minding my own business you know just got back from a date felt like I was on top of the world...I woke up the next morning did everything I needed then left my house to see smoke. Me being The Creator I ran down to see what's going on when I got closer, I saw guys in like glass armor it was all black and glossy. I fought a couple of the guys after that the big bad came out from the shadows. His name is Vulcan he stood out like flowers in a wasteland his armor was like molten lava glowing like it to. I was too cocky...thought I could beat him no problem turns out I couldn't beat him in the process lost everything now I'm here" I said to the kid trying to sum up all that happened

"Wow I would have never seen a man like you rule a planet...all the things that happened to you how are you still alive after all that" the kid said amazed

“Not giving up on myself and others on top of that people are always going to take what’s yours no matter how big or small” I told the kid

“But why” the kid said confused

“Because they are not capable of creating some so great themselves so they take from others and call it their own” I tell the kid

“Wow sir I can’t believe there are people like that in the universe” the kid said shocked

“More than you could imagine kid...the universe is filled with negatives but there are still a lot of positives if you take the time to search for them”

“How can you tell sir”

“You’ll just know kid...you’ll just know” I said to the kid

“Wow sir I really hope to be like you one day” the kid said to me

“You can be better than me if you put your mind to it kid...now you best be getting home it getting dark”

“It will take me awhile to get home...my village is a day’s walk” the kid said

“Well lucky for you I have a portal over that way” I said walking the way to the portal

“A portal?” The kid said confused

“Yes, a portal now hurry”

We both walked to the portal which was only 5 minutes from where we were. I had the portal scan for a nearby village eventually it picked up the boy’s village. We both walked through the portal on the other side was this beautiful wooden village in the middle of the forest. Houses were built in trees with bridges connecting them there were stairs so they could get down if need be. The center of the village was a big wooden building if I had to guess it would be like the white house.

“So where are your parents or house” I asked the kid

“This way sir”

I followed the kid of the wooden stairs and walked across about 8 bridges intill we got to the boy’s house. I knocked on the wooden door when I did the door opened a few seconds later.

“Oh my god Alalun your back me and your father were worried about you” the boy’s mother said

“I’m okay mom I promise...this man helped me home” the boy said

“You helped my son home” the mother said as she looked at me

“I did yes” I said to the mother

"Thank you so much it means a lot to me and his father" the mother said tearing up

"Also don't worry he won't be running away anytime soon I promise you that" I said to the mother

"I hope so" the mother said looking at her son

"Before I go, I want you to have this kid" I have him my somewhat damaged helmet

"But...but why" the kid said surprised

"To give you a sense of hope and a reminder even when times get tough you always get back up like I told you I did" I said to the kid

"Who are you" the mother said confused

"I'm The Creator ma'am...I hope you guys have a wonderful rest of your night" I said to them and walked back to the opened portal

When I got to the portal, I looked at the city one last time and said in a whisper

" I'm getting mine back"

Chapter 4
The War pt. 1

This war it's going to last awhile I know that or maybe it won't who knows but I'm ready for fight. My training led me to this moment and I'm ready to finally face it. Being on the Peace Planet was eye opening also something I needed. For once in my life, I felt free like nothing mattered to me...that feeling is something I'll never forget. Scarlet showed up in her ship to pick me up from the Peace Planet. I stayed on the Peace Planet for over a month to really be focused and prepared for anything. We arrived at Earth 2 and what I was met with was completely horrid. Earth 2 was all lava like all the building were rebuilt out of some black stone glowing orange like lava. The water was replaced with lava some of the fountains were destroyed because of the lava.

"Scarlet what did they do to my creation" I said in an emotional tone

"Jordan this is worse than we thought" Scarlet said looking at me scared

"Scarlet I was put through hell for months I was beaten down for months...this...this is not going to stop me from take my creation back...on top of that my people look up to me so I am going to do this...the right way" I told Scarlet very confidently

"You can't go down there are you crazy...That down there is a terrible idea Jordan" Scarlet yelled

"Listen you're the one who said I could do this okay...I'm confident that I can do this with or without people on my side" I told Scarlet while staring into her eyes

Scarlet flew the ship down to the landing pad areas when we landed, I walked out. There were guys everywhere almost patrolling the area. When they saw who walked out of the ship, they ran over to me with their swords drawn.

"Stand down Creator" the one guard said

"Really guys we are going to do this" I said laughing a bit

"DOWN NOW" the other guard yelled

"Ughh fine if it shuts you up".

I turned around got on my knees and put my hands on my head. The guards walked over when the one guard grabbed my arm, I did a backflip while holding the guy's rist. I slammed him onto his back when I did, I kicked the other guy's leg making him fall face first onto the ground.

"Scarlet, do I have an extra helmet in there" I yelled to Scarlet

"I think so" Scarlet said looking for one

"I'm sure I left one in there" I said

"Yeah, here it's your old one" Scarlet said throwing it to me

"Thank you and yeah it will be fine I used the same helmet design" I said to Scarlet

"Of course, now do you want me to tell snake eyes to send his men"

"No, not yet I'll let you know keep your ear piece in at all times please"

"I will Jordan...I guess I'll see you soon"

"Indeed, you will" I said as we kissed goodbye

I started to make my way to the tower to find Vulcan who probably thinks I'm dead. As I was walking to the tower guards flooded the streets all armed with swords. Then from out of the crowd of guards Vulcan emerged looking like he did when we last fought

"So, The Creator back from the dead huh to claim what's his" Vulcan said enjoying every second

"Yes, you are right I'm here to take back what's mine...this time I will kill you and take everything away from you...like you did me" I said angerly

"I'm not so sure you have the balls to do that Creator"

"You really don't think so...look what happened to the last person who tried to take my world...hes dead as will you very soon I promise you that"

"Bold statement their Creator...I'm holding you to that promise" Vulcan said with a smile that you could just hear

I put two fingers to my left ear to activate the coms.

"Scarlet its time send them all" I said quietly

"Copy that" Scarlet said back

Ships started to fill the sky as they all landed behind me one by one.

"Let's do this" I said to myself

Vulcan looked a bit scared when all the ships landed. So, seeing Vulcan like that I started to run toward him and his guards. When I got close a guard tackled me back as he did Vulcan ran into the tower. I kicked the guard off of me while he was on the ground, I snapped his neck. Scarlet ran up to me to see if I was okay.

"Hey you okay Jordan" Scarlet said

"Yeah, I'm fine...Vulcan ran into the tower it's going to be impossible to get in there by just walking in" I said trying to think of something

"So, what do you propose we do about that" Scarlet said

"Okay when the time comes, you're going to fly me up there in a ship to my office...ill climb onto my balcony and break the glass to get in if the door is locked...then improvise from there" I said to Scarlet

"Why not right now" Scarlet said confused

"We got to take some of the guards out even with all of our guys it's going to be impossible to get a ship up there without being shot down" I said to Scarlet

"Okay then let's do this" Scarlet said

We started to fight some of the guards but it felt like there were unlimited guards. We were all getting tired so we all made a bit of a barrier so we could get a bit of a break. We had guys watching just in case some guards tried something.

"This is bullshit I won't be able to get up there in time or at all if we don't do something about these lava bitches" I yelled

"Kid this is a war it won't solve its self in an hour" Chapel said to me

"Plus, we don't have anything to use...they have everything" Scarlet said to me

"Well, there's one thing we could get that would help...I was reading about it before all this happened" I said to Scarlet and Chapel

"What is it kid" Chapel said

"It's called a Galactic Core...it's filled with elemental power...Earth Energy, fire Energy, water Energy, air Energy, dark matter Energy, Void Energy, All-knowing Energy, Black Hole Energy, and Gama Ray Burst Energy... All these can be formed into one to be the most powerful thing in the entire universe... Thing is we only know where the Earth one is but I think I know who has the fire one" I explained to them both

"Kid I don't think messing with all of this is a good idea this sounds dangerous and you know that danger was my thing but this...all this is a new level for me" Chapel said

"Chapel, if Vulcan is cheating then why can't we even the playing field we will lose more lives and on top of that your guys lives as well" I said

"But kid that doesn't mean you have to cheat as well...your powerful enough to kill him and yet you want to make yourself powerful for fun" Chapel said

“Yes, if he has one either way ill have one so they are better in my hands then Vulcan” I said

“If you lose then Vulcan will have two...Vulcan will be the most powerful being in the universe” Chapel said worried

“Chapel, we trained for a reason, right?... I know I can beat him I’m not going to be cocky about it”

I told Chapel trying to convince him

“Ugh kid...please be careful I don’t need to lose you” Chapel said to me

“Chapel, you won’t lose me...I promise” I said as I gave Chapel a hug

“I’m going with Jordan” Scarlet said

“Woah no you’re not...I need you here more than with me” I said shocked Scarlet even said that

“No, I’m coming with you”

“Scarlet, you’re staying here that’s the end of it plus someone needs to watch Chapels back” I said as a joke

We all agreed that I’d be the only one going to find the Earth Core it allows you to control everything on an Earth like planet. I took off into the universe following what the book told me to do. Honestly would have been easier if there was a map but that would have been too easy. The planet is small almost like the Moon but a bit bigger also it’s a very reddish planet. Plants are red the water is a dark purple and the clouds are a soft pink color so I got to look out for a planet matching what I just remembered from the book. I had to travel 685 billion lightyears to get to the galaxy where this planet is supposably at. Something could have changed in the galaxy well many things could have changed by now depending on when the book was writing but hoping this will be easy. Eventually I got the galaxy and the system that this planet was in was not far away from where I was. I could see a red planet from a distance so I was hoping to God that this was the planet I was looking for. I flew my ship down the planet and landed in a forest in the middle of nowhere. The book never mentioned any sort of civilization which means this is going to be harder to find this core. I started to walk through the red leafed forest just thinking about a lot but also focusing on finding this core.

“Being alone on this planet feels...so nice but so frighting” I said out loud

“I understand how you feel human” A voice said from all around me

“Umm am I crazy or did I just hear someone”

“you’re not crazy human...I’m all around you at all times”

“Let me guess the Earth Core?”

“Yes, it is the Earth Core human...also that’s what you seek I assume”

“Yeah, it is what I seek...it’s only to do good not for destruction”

“I’ve heard that before human I killed everyone who I thought I could trust with the core...they all said they would do good but they used it to destroy planets and create terrible planets with terrible beings on them”

"I understand I really do...but I'm telling the truth someone has the Fire Core and hes destroying my world and killing my people...if that's not a good enough reason then I don't really care but I know it's the truth"

"If this is true, I'll be taking a big risk giving you this power and trusting a stranger that needs it more than I do for once it's a hard decision"

"If I don't use it the way you want it to be used then kill me, I don't care but I do know that my friends, family, and people need my help".

The man formed in front of me he was very old from the looks of it. The man had a golden robe on with white designs all over it. His shirt was a dirt brown but looked very soft. The pants were very loose very free not anchored to his ankle's. The color of his pants where white and he didn't have shoes on.

"Well then, I really hope you do good human the universe really needs it" the man said with a smile

"Trust me I'm going to do all the good I can sir I can assure you that" I said as I put my hand out for a handshake

"I trust you..."

"I'm The Creator"

"Huh weird name but...I trust you Creator" The man shook my hand

"Good luck creator I hope you get your planet back because you deserve to have that planet of yours" the man said as he disappeared

"Damn I wish I was able to do that"

The core was where he disappeared the core is pretty big like a size of a plate. It was glowing a very nice golden brown the inside looked like water was flowing in the Core. After I grabbed it, I took it onto the ship and started to make my way back to Earth 2.

Chapter 5
The War pt. 2

I finally got to Earth 2 with the core I brought it over to Chapel and Scarlet.

“Hey, I got the core guys...but I don’t know how to use it” I said to them

“You’re kidding me right” Scarlet said to me

“Kid how do you not know how to use it” chapel said looking at me crazy

“I will figure it out don’t worry”

I sat down with the core in my hands trying to think on how the core works.

“Jordan maybe you should try and have it form around your suit” Chapel said

“I don’t think that would work...it seems too easy” I said looking at chapel

“Worth a try kid”.

I deactivated my suit when I did, I had chapel hold it on my back. I activated my suit and the core stayed when my suit connected to the helmet, I could feel the power of the core in my body. My suit started to glow a bright yellow in the crevices of the suit.

“Did it work kid” chapel said running over to me

“Yeah, it definitely worked Chapel” I said as I fell to a knee

I could feel planets around me almost like they were living beings. I saw their pasts their future it’s all just amazing but sad at the same time. These feelings I was feeling from my Earth were screams for help it really made me cry but also it made me angry.

“Kid are you okay...what’s going on” Chapel said holding my shoulder

“Jordan are you okay...Chapel is the power too much to handle” Scarlet said to Chapel worried

"No, he should be fine...I mean he looks it" "Guys I'm fine...I just needed a minute...to take what I felt all in" I said standing up

"What happened Jordan" Scarlet said to me

"I understood and felt all the planets around me almost like I knew them personally for trillions of years...Earth 2 is slowly dying from what Vulcan is doing I can feel that" I said to them both

"So, what you have powers now" Scarlet said confused

"No, they will come to me when I need them the most".

After I said that we started to get attacked by Vulcans men.

"We need to go now" chapel yelled

"Scarlet it's time for the plan" I said

Scarlet nodded and we both ran to the ship we both got onto the ship. I got myself ready to jump out of the back of the ship. We flew up to where my office balcony is when we did, I opened the back. When I opened it, I was about to jump out but the ship started to lose control.

"WE HAVE BEEN HIT" Scarlet yelled.

I was flung out of the back of the ship into a glass pane on the 426th floor of The Tower. I was badly injured from the fall into the building. Getting up was hard to do but I did so I could see if Scarlet got out in time before the ship hit the ground. The explosion of the ship was when I knew she had to be dead I fell back in shock I couldn't feel anything.

"So sad Creator I truly am... but you did this to yourself and to her" Vulcan said walking closer to me

"you son of a... bitch I'm going to...kill you" I said getting up

"No, you won't Creator...your broken more than you have been in a while"

"Trust me you son of a bitch you're going to die slowly and painfully"

"Wow I'm so scared Creator...I really am".

I stumbled toward him as we walked toward me. I ducked at his punch and kicked him back into a desk. As he fell back onto the desk, I held him up by his throat and slammed him into the desk. I picked him up as he was up, I started to throw punches to his helmet over and over. It started to crack but before I could break it, he kicked me back and punched my ribs which were broken from the fall. After that he dislocated my left knee. Vulcan picked me up by the neck and stabbed me with his sword it went all the way through.

"You lose again Creator...you lost your friends, your girlfriend, your family, and most important of them all you lost your world...seems like you lose more then you win" Vulcan said as I was holding onto him

"Not...to...today...Vulcan".

I grabbed him and pulled him out the window with me. We both started to free fall down to the ground as we were I pulled the sword out of my chest. After that I started to make my way to Vulcan in the air and I was able to grab ahold of him and have him hit the ground first. We both just laid there for a bit but my healing kicked in after a while and I got up. After I got up so did, he and we staired at each other. We ran towards each other as we did, I kicked him to the ground. He got up quickly and was able to tackle me to the ground. Vulcan started to pound on my somewhat healed ribs. I kneed him off me so I could get up and prepare for his next attack. As I got up, I felt power hit me and a boost of energy filled my body. I ran toward Vulcan kicking him in the face I cut his right leg and then his left arm when he tried to punch me. After my kick to his face Vulcans helmet was cracked a lot more, I could almost see his face. I picked him up by his shoulder and just looked at him through my somewhat broken helmet.

"You took a lot from me but now I get to take most of it back today... you lost Vulcan and I can't wait to see you slowly die as you watch your army fall" I said to Vulcan showing I wasn't scared of him anymore

"You will always be a failure Creator...no matter how hard you train no matter how...hard you learn from your past you will always be haunted by these days... and let me tell you this...is just the beginning" Vulcan said as he laughed at the last part of his sentence

I stabbed Vulcan through the center of his chest so he could die a slow death. As he fell, I took his helmet off and when I did, I wanted to take back what I've just done.

"Vixen, what...why...why did you do this...how could you do this to me" I fell to my knees

"Jordan, you created something beyond what anyone thought possible and I wanted it kid" My uncle said shedding a tear

"Jordan I really didn't want to do this to you...I really didn't but I had no choice" My uncle said again

"Vixen, you had a choice but you...you acted like that choice was never an option...you chose destruction and murder over your only family" I said taking my helmet off and putting it to the side

"I know Jordan but... now I'm getting what...I deserve...death" my uncle said losing his breath

"No, what you deserve is a second chance but I can't give that to you now and I'm sorry that I couldn't help sooner" I said tearing up

"Men like me...don't deserve second chances Jordan........Goodbye my nephew......I love you" my uncle said before passing away

"I love you to Vixen".

I shut his eyes out of respect even though Vixen took everything from me.

"Hey kid...are you okay...did you take out Vulcan" Chapel said

"Yeah, I did...he was my uncle" I said to chapel tearing up

"Kid...I'm so sorry but also, he did deserve what he got" Chapel said

"Chapel, he didn't deserve to die...I know he did some terrible things but he didn't deserve this...I could have helped him through all this" I said to Chapel

"Kid he ruined your life and you just don't care at all" Chapel said to me

"You really don't understand do you Chapel he was the only family I had left...he turned evil and I could have stopped that I was just too busy that I didn't see the signs" I said to Chapel

"Because we have a blind spot for family...I did so do most people in the universe" Chapel said

"Did anyone find Scarlets remains or do I have to do that" I said crying at the thought of seeing her dead

"We found her and she's still breathing we are having her moved to a hospital of world for the best treatment" Chapel said

"How is she alive...I saw the ship explode" I yelled

"She was close to dying but she will be okay" Chapel said

"Oh my god this day it's been a weird one I'll say that" I said looking up at the tower

"Hey kid the core...I didn't see you use it" Chapel said curious

"It didn't need to be used" I said to Chapel

"What do you mean it didn't need to be used" Chapel said confused

"The core it only can be used when it needs to be used the most...the core knew I would win the fight somehow and it didn't give me the power" I said to Chapel

"See kid I told you that you didn't need the core to win the fight...also did he have the Fire Core" Chapel said to me

"Yes, he did it was in my office I saw it before the ship went down" I said to chapel

"Can I trust you with these Cores kid" "I'd say no but I think this proves I can be trusted with them"

"Alright I agree kid but go see Scarlet, she needs you right now"

"What about the little mess we caused" I laughed when I said that

"Yeah, the little mess kid...don't worry about it I will take care of it"

"You sure Chapel I can stay behind and help"

"Like I said Scarlet needs you"

"Yeah, but she has surgery so I'm sure I'll have time to help"

"Damn it kid just go" Chapel said laughing

"Fine old man I will" I laughed as I gave him a hug

"You did good kid"

"No, you did good Chapel, you helped me... you helped a lot and I thank you from the bottom of my heart"

"Jordan you are the strongest kid I know...you don't see it at all but I see through your suit you have so much more to learn but won't let yourself because your scared of failure"

"You could say failure is my weakness but you are right but you showed me I can fail but still win"

"Isn't that what a Sensei does kid" Chapel said as he hands me my helmet

"Yeah, they teach"

After Chapel and I were done talking I went to see Scarlet at the hospital. On my way to the hospital, I was just thinking to myself that I did it I really overcame a challenge. Only if my mom was here to see this, she would be proud of me. I always think to myself what could have been if my mom was still here how much she could have helped me. Being The Creator, it means a lot but also is a very difficult job more difficult than you could ever imagine. I've lost so many people already which I don't want to happen but it's part of the journey. I got to the hospital just in time she was out of surgery and recovering in one of the rooms. I asked for her room number and when I was given the room number, I bolted to see her.

"Knock, knock it's me" I said as I entered the room

"Hey it's you" Scarlet said in a very raspy voice and exhausted voice

"I'm very happy to see you...you really scared me out there" I said trying to just brighten the mood

"I missed you so much...did we win" Scarlet said coughing

"Yeah...yeah, we won" I said while thinking of all that happened

"Chapel is he..." Scarlet said as she teared up

"He's alive don't worry" I said sitting on the edge of the bed

"I thought I was dead Jordan" She said tearing up

"So did I Scarlet...I heard the explosion and thought the worst" I said tearing up

"I'm just thankful someone pulled me out in time"

"Hey you will have a pretty cool scar though alone with an amazing story" I said to make her laugh

"Oh, my you with your jokes I missed them" Scarlet said chuckling

"I love you Scarlet" I said before kissing her head

"I love you to Jordan".

I stayed with Scarlet for a couple more hours in till she went back to bed. Being there with Scarlet it felt like years have gone by but it was just hours. I feel like we haven't had this time of time to ourselves in a long time. Honestly reminds me of when we were just talking for the first time on Earth 1.

"Hey man you doing alright" Jay said walking into the room

"I'm doing alright man how are you doing" I said to Jay with a forced smile

"You sure man you look kinda lost man" Jay said to me

"Maybe I am lost Jay I really don't know anymore...after the war it's kinda been hard" I said to jay

"Hey listen Jordan you did good alright...better than all of us" Jay said trying to make me feel good

"Jay, I know there will be more people like my uncle out there maybe stronger than my uncle and I have to be better than I was today" I said with fear in my eyes

"Jordan, you will have a team behind you always and no matter what...we aren't going to leave you like we did man it was screwed up all three of us knew but didn't care" Jay said

"I know we screwed up but I also don't want us to be surrounded by secrets everything about Earth 2 is made to give people hope and a destiny to follow...honestly, I was chasing after perfection which even I should have known isn't possible" I said to Jay

"We all do man once in our life we search for perfection but I'll leave you go man just wanted to check up on you"

"Thanks man I really missed you guys and I'm glad you came back" I said smiling

"Me to" Jay walked out of the room and Scarlet turned to me

"Your right Jordan it's not possible...no matter what...perfection will never truly exist" Scarlet said with her hand on my cheek

"Hey you were supposed to be asleep"

"Well, I wasn't I heard everything Jordan" Scarlet said giggling

"Well, I have something in the works it's meant to help more people since Earth 2 is getting crowded" I said as I hold Scarlet's hand on my cheek

"What is this project Jordan"

"It's called The System...a way to bring more planets into our solar system. We were going to have hundreds of planets all different environments but all habitable" I said with a smile

"You really put thought into this Jordan...like a lot of thought"

"Yeah, I did put a lot of thought into this...just need to be able to make it happen is all. Making Earth 2 was a lot of work and lots of time I'm just trying to find a way to just make that easier and quicker" I said to Scarlet

"I know you will find a way love you always do" Scarlet said with a smile

After talking with Scarlet, I went home to get some rest in my bed. When I got home, I saw a circular device on my counter. I went over to the counter as I did, I was being very careful just in case it was a bomb. When I got close a hologram appeared a little bit above the device. It was my brother that appeared as the hologram.

"If you are watching this brother that means you killed Vulcan better known as our uncle. Yes, I knew he was Vulcan and yes, I was the one who sent him to take over your Earth for me. I told you I would be back but you only talked about your suit being better well I hope you are now taking this seriously. We won't stop trying and I know you won't stop protecting but one day you will fall... and we will rise to a point where even you won't be able to stop us. Be prepared Creator for hell to finally be released on your precious Earth 2"

The hologram ended when it did, I was filled with anger but in shock at the same time. My brother will pay for this...this time I will kill him no more mercy will be given from me. Every time I give mercy, they come back but not this time.

Chapter 6
Core Collector

The planet Omicron Persei, named so for its similarities to the fictional version, is an earth-like planet in a fairly small solar system with ten other planets. Omicron Persei is about 1.6 times bigger than Earth and its gravity is about 1.96 times that of Earth. A single day lasts 48.31 hours and a year lasts 267 days. The planet is made up of 14 continents, which make up 59% of the planet's landmass. 5 moons orbit the planet and Omicron Persei itself orbits a white sun in an almost perfectly circular orbit. The planet is all forest except the beaches While flowers, shrubs do exist, fungi are nowhere to be found. The water is a dark purple with a bit of fog on the top. The sun is a nice orange red throughout the whole day. When it is dark there is a constant eclipse going which provides little light during the night. The glow is a rose red which honestly looks amazing I wanted Earth 2 to look something like this but it's not possible. Anyways this is where the Black Hole Core is located. You're most likely wondering how I now know this information well let me tell you. There have been rumors going around about someone finding cores left and right. Now me being me I'm thinking the worst this person could be wanting them to make the Galactic Core which can kill the universe and everyone in it. Basically, giving the universe a new start very early in its life but if there is a way to not make that happen and instead of the universe dying what about making all evil die. Yes, it's a very screwed up plan but saving the universe is the main thing so taking the people who want to destroy it out of the universe is how we save it.

"Jordan, I think this may be a bad idea" Hesh said

"Well Jordan does have a good idea just not the best way of doing it" Jay said

"But this is the best way...everyone we faced I killed them except my brother and now he wants to keep sending people after me" I said to Hesh and Jay

"There has to be another way Jordan" Hesh said

"Hesh the last attack hurt all of us in our own unique ways" Jay said to Hesh

"Yeah, I could have lost Scarlet because of my brother and you want to say there's another way" I said to Hesh

“I really don’t know how it feels to almost loose someone like a girlfriend or wife but we are the heroes Jordan...heroes don’t kill they grant mercy” Hesh said to me

“Hesh this isn’t a movie where they will just stop because the hero granted them mercy...I did that to my brother and now hes sending people after me” I said to Hesh

“Guys lets calm down okay we all have mixed feelings about this but we also have someone out there collecting the cores so we need to focus on this person. Intill we get to the point where your brother is here fighting us then we can figure this out together” Jay said to both of us

“Yeah, your right but do we even have anything to go off of except the Black Hole Core” Hesh said

“Yeah, I found the planet on which its located...I don’t know about you two but I’m going right now so we don’t waste any time” I said to Hesh and Jay

“Well let’s get ready for an adventure then” Jay said

“I always love a deadly adventure” Hesh said laughing

“Who doesn’t” I said laughing

We all got ready when we were done, we all met at the ship. We loaded everything we needed for the trip when that was done, we started the journey into the stars.

“So, how is Scarlet man” Jay said sitting next to me in the cockpit

“Shes doing better she has to learn to walk again...that really made her upset when she couldn’t feel her legs” I said to Jay

“Damn man I’m sorry to hear that” Jay said to me

“It’s alright man she’s strong...but have you met anyone yet” I said laughing a bit

“Ugh man...yeah, I did after our fight we met in a coffee shop” Jay said to me smile like he was reliving the day

“Thats great man...what’s her name”

“Her name is Avery and she is the best”

“I’m glad to hear that Jay I really am”

“Thanks man I appreciate it I really do”

“Well man are you guys dating or still just friends”

“Uhh that’s...kinda hard to say right now”

“What makes you say that”

“Well, I’m sure she likes me because she flirts and I do the same but we haven’t asked each other”

“what’s stopping you man”

“Well, the day I was going to ask is the day the war started so I went to fight beside you”

“Dude, you didn’t have to skip out on a date basically...you knew I would have been fine”

“To Scarlet you didn’t seem to think you had it...so yes, I did have to skip my date to be with my friend who needed me”

“Well after this is all over, you’re going to ask her even if something happens...okay”

“I will try man...kinda have to build the confidence back up”

“Oh my god come on man...you’re a badass fighter who fought people better than the three of us also had an Earth blow up and you’re telling me your scared to ask a girl out”

“Dude how about you fuck off okay it’s scary” Jay said laughing

“Dude come on if you get rejected its whatever there’s like trillions upon trillions of girls in the universe”

“Yeah, I know but it’s like a connection you and Scarlet have I don’t want to lose something so good”

“I get that man I really do but if you hold back your whole life you will always hold yourself back from every decision your faced with” I said as I grabbed Jays shoulder

“Jordan, it’s hard to make decisions like you do I’m not as brave as you” Jay said looking down a bit

“Jay, you’re brave you truly are you fight in every battle...knowing it could be your last fight now that sounds brave to me” I said as I looked at Jay and nodded at him

“I guess your right” Jay said looking up and taking a big breath in

We eventually got to the planet Omicron Persei we landed on the beach since that’s the only open landing spot we could find. The ocean was beautiful along with the breeze that came with the waves. The sky orange red mixed with bits of purple was honestly the coolest thing I’ve seen in a while. The planets were orange but a very faded or weathered orange. The bark of the trees are white but again if it was weathered or faded.

“Well seems like we found a fucking gold mine guys” Hesh said out loud

“Could you watch your language please” I said to Hesh

“Whatever man” Hesh said back

“I mean just look at this planet it’s so beautiful so...peaceful and quiet” Jay said taking everything in

“I know she’s a beauty...fun fact I was going to make Earth 2 something like this” I said to Hesh and Jay

“Why didn’t you” Hesh said

"It can't be created it needs to happen naturally which is very rare" I said to Hesh and Jay

"Well damn it would have been an amazing site to wake up to every morning though" Jay said

"Oh, just wait intill dark guys it gets way better" I said laughing

"What do you mean by that are we going to kill some big ass monster or little tiny monsters" Hesh says jokingly

"Maybe I've never been here before but I can say no its something different" I said while working on finding the core

I was scanning for high energy levels all around the planet which worked but we had to somehow get to the place it wants us to go to.

"So, I found the core but it's in the densest part of the forest" I said to Hesh and Jay

"Well of course it is why would who ever put it there make it easy" Hesh said

"True higher beings make it harder for people like us" Jay said

"Okay what do you mean by people like us... we basically are higher beings" I said to Jay

"Hey let's focus on the core please" Hesh said

"Since when did you care about doing work" I said to Hesh

"Yeah, honestly since when did you care" Jay says

"Okay can we talk about this later" Hesh said laughing a bit

We all started to walk into the forest which I'm used to but this forest was different. The forest felt very heavy like some shit went down here years ago.

"Guys is it just me or does the forest feel very dark and heavy" I said to Hesh and Jay

"Yeah, it feels sad like very sad" Jay said choking on his words

"What the hell happened here" Hesh said tearing up

"I don't know but it feels powerful...maybe it was the core" I said as I looked around

"What...what do you see" Hesh said

"I'm feeling drawn this way for some reasons" I said as I started to walk toward the energy I was feeling

We all started to feel the pressure that I was feeling a bit ago but it got heavier as we got closer to it. The feeling of our skin being ripped off as we got closer to what we think is the core grew more and more. We all saw this circle of just grassland with rocks, trees, grass, and star dust all floating around a throne.

“Is that our guy” Jay said not taking his eyes off him

“Well, I’m guessing it is hes the guy sitting on a throne” Hesh said Joking as usual

I started to walk closer but stopped as I got to where the circle started.

“The Creator of Earth 2 on my planet...how lucky am I” The man in the throne said to me

“Yeah, your lucky day I guess” I said to the man but he never turned around to know it was me

“I know why you’re here Creator” The man said gazing out into the stars

“That obvious huh” I said not really surprised

“You know I can’t give you something so dangerous Creator” He said like he said this trillions of times

“Thats why I’m here so they never fall into the wrong hands...so I can truly be The Creator. I only protect people I don’t start wars for fun its chaotic and foolish”

“I know I’ve watched the things you’ve done through the eyes of the black holes... you’re a very interesting man Creator you really are...so are your two friends. You have good friends Creator you really do” The man said like he knew them

“Yes, they are great friends always have been” I said wondering why hes getting off the core subject

“Creator can I truly trust you with Black Hole Core” he said then stood up

“Yes, id sacrifice my life to protect the core” I said to him with pure confidence behind my words

The man turned around with the core in his hands. He started to walk down to me as he did, I could see him more and more clear. The man has a very nice leather jacket on it was all white. His shirt was light grey along with is pants having a mix of both white and grey. His shoes were just grey but he looked like a true god even though he was dressed so weird.

“Then I entrust you with my core Creator” he said smiling at me

“Thank you, sir I appreciate it,” I said smiling but he couldn’t see it because of my helmet

“Make the universe safe Creator...like we never could”

“I will try my damn best sir I promise you that” I said as we both hugged

“Now I’m afraid it’s time for me to move on”

“Move on?” I said confused

“Yes, move on to another life in another universe...goodbye Creator”

The man said as he faded away into thin air, I was left in shock that he just left to go to a new universe. I had my theories but I really couldn’t believe that there were other universes out there.

"Did you get the core" Hesh said as he was walking closer to me

"Yeah, I got it...guys I just found out something crazy" I said still in shock

"What did you find out Jordan" Jay said confused

"The theory of other universes that I had for the longest time...trying to prove it to everyone but I couldn't...well he just proved it to me" I said so happily and so emotional

"Wait other universes exist...dude you were right" Hesh said so shocked as well

"I can see Earth 1 again and see my mom again" I said tearing up

"Maybe right now isn't the best time to do something like that maybe sometime in the future" Jay said holding my shoulder

"Yeah, your right man...one day I will"

We all started to walk back to the ship when we got there, we packed up everything onto the ship. We all decided to stick around a bit for the view also so we could talk about our lives and not about work.

"You know it's been a while since we have done this" Jay said after taking his helmet off

"Yeah, last time was at the nest on Earth 1" Hesh said after taking his helmet off

"Geez talk about a through back am I right...the nest seems so distant" I said placing my helmet in the sand

"Yeah, it does but it also seems like just yesterday we had our last meet up there" Jay said

"You're not wrong man you're really not" Hesh said

"Well hopefully one day we will get to see it again" I said putting the core next to my helmet

"Yeah, it would be great to see the nest one more time" Hesh said smiling

"Guys do you ever think we will live normal lives again" Jay said wondering

"No, probably not" I said laughing

"Oh my god...okay do you really think we will" Jay said laughing as well

"Well, that's up to us right I'm going to choose when I can finally live and not have to watch over Earth 2 anymore" I said while looking up to the stars

"Well, I'm sure our time will come when we are all ready to actually live and not want to be at war for eternity" Hesh said

"Yeah, I really don't want to be fighting my whole life...I wanna have kids and grow old" Jay said

“Yeah, me to but I don’t think I could bring myself to have kids” I said looking down shaking my head

“Why not isn’t that your dream” Hesh said to me

“Yeah, it was but let’s be honest we will never defeat all the evil that plague’s this universe... bringing kids into it and not knowing if I can protect them if something happens you know...I couldn’t live with myself” I said to both of them

“Geez man that’s dark as hell but understandable” Hesh said to me

“Doesn’t mean you should give up Jordan” Jay said to me

“It kinda does I can’t have a kid because of the universe and all the bad people in it who want my home” I said tearing up

“Hey we will change the universe Jordan its possible” Hesh said trying to help

“One day it may but there will always be threats Hesh there always will be...We can only do so much to stop them but eventually we will go down one of these days trying” I said then got up and got into the ship

“Damn he really has a shitty view on the universe” Hesh said to Jay

“I’m surprised you don’t yet man” Jay said to Hesh

“I mean it can always be changed Jay...Other parts of the universe don’t know about us and we probably don’t know about them so who knows what’s out there” Hesh said to Jay

“What’s your point Hesh” Jay snapped at Hesh

“Hey calm down why are you getting snappy for” Hesh said confused

“Just explain your point please” Jays said

“Okay...my point is they could be beyond good but we don’t know that so why don’t we show them that we exist give them hope. Every bad person has a reason to go all stabby, stabby you know” Hesh explained to Jay

“So, what you’re saying is bring them to Earth 2 and basically have them live there so they won’t experience bad shit” Jay asked Hesh

“Yeah basically”

“Dude then they won’t learn what it feels like to lose...they will think they are on top of the world and do bad shit anyway...we lose either way Jordan was right about that” Jay explained to Hesh again

“Oh, my your...your right we can’t get around that” Hesh said realizing

“Let’s just get home man I’m exhausted” Jay said to Hesh.

We got onto our ship and we all went home to Earth 2. When we got back, I put the cores in a secret hiding spot. It was in my office somewhere even if they did find it by sheer luck, they would need me to open it so they are protected. So where does this leave us honestly, I don't know everything seemed to be going great but those are the famous last words.

Chapter 7
Fracture In Time

3 years have passed in my life in those 3 years lots have happened. Scarlet convinced me to have kids. We have a daughter and a son my daughter's name is Athena and my sons name is Link. Athena is older than Link by a year but aging works very different on Earth 2. Athena is 3 but she has the body of a teenager Link is behind her a bit but they are basically the same height. They stop aging fast at 18 which means everything will begin happing normally instead of rapidly.

"Crazy universe out there am I right" Scarlet said to me

"Yeah, very crazy baby...I just can't believe our kids are living in it" I said to Scarlet as I looked up at the stars

"Well, I'm glad they are living on the most protected planet in the whole universe" Scarlet said smiling at me

"Well, when they are old enough hopefully, they will do the same when we are gone" I said smiling back at Scarlet

"They will be the greatest fighters in the whole universe like us baby" Scarlet said to me

"You mean like you I just protect everyone" I said laughing

"You're kidding me right" She laughed back

"I mean we both are pretty good fighters but our kids definitely will beat our asses for sure" I laughed more

"Hey dad can you read me a bedtime story please...pretty please" Athena said walking into our room

"Of course, my little firebird...come on" I said holding Athena's hand back to her room

I walked her back to her room. When we got to her room, I picked her up and put her on her bed. I pulled the covers up to her chest and tucked it under her.

“You were about to jump into the portal to Earth 2” Athena said smiling

“Thats right...okay so I jumped through the portal as I did, I felt good that I helped those people live. As I came out of the portal though that was a different story. I felt so alive but also so afraid because of what was to come. Seeing the bright sun with all those different hues of orange, red, and yellow, gave me strength and hope. The people that I just saved were looking to me for answers on what to do next. So, I gave them the houses that were already made. One problem solved became 3 more unsolved ones. We had barley any food and so we went to a whole new world...but that will have to wait intill next time” I said to Athena then got up from the stool

“Please dad just a little more of the story...please” Athena said trying to convince me

“Not today my little firebird but next time I promise” I said to Athena then gave her a kiss on the forehead

“Awww okay dad...goodnight I love you” Athena said

“Goodnight Athena, I love you to” I said to her then turned her light off and shut the door behind me

I walked to the bedroom where Scarlet was reading a book in bed. I climbed into bed and laid my head on the pillow and went to sleep. The next morning came quick I was awoken by Athena and Link saying to make breakfast. Scarlet just laid in bed and told me to deal with the kids.

“Okay guys let’s go what do you guys want today egg, waffles, or pancakes” I said laughing and kidding around with them

“All three of them of course dad” Link said laughing

“Yeah, I agree all three sounds good to me” Athena said agreeing with link

“Oh, you guys are a pain in the ass sometimes you know that I said laughing more but all three-coming right up”

I started making breakfast for everyone as I did, I got a knock at the first door. I asked Scarlet to take over as I went to get the door.

I opened the door to see Jay

“Hey everything alright man” I said to jay

“No, we have a big problem and we need you in right now” Jay said with a scared tone “Alright give me a bit and I’ll be right in don’t worry” I said to Jay

I went to the bedroom to activate my suit when I did, I told Scarlet I had to go to the office. As I entered the office everyone had a picture of someone in my suit on the big screen.

"What the hell how did this person get one of my suits" I yelled out loud

"They didn't nothing was ever stolen from The Tower...No one else can make it like you did which is where it gets worse" Hesh said to me

"That person right there is you but not from this universe" Jay said to me

"Wait so me from another universe is now here for what" I said confused

"Well, he was seen leaving a planet with the Dark Energy Core" Jay said scared

"I'm guessing he's going to use them to do bad" I said with my arms crossed

"Yeah, he killed everyone to get the core even the core keeper" Jay said again

I walked into my office just with the feeling of losing it all...this time I felt like its either life or death there is no in the middle. I will either die or my twin will die this is going to be the hardest fight of my life.

"Jordan you okay" Jay said

"No, not really man...I just found out that other me is trying to end my universe. How would you be feeling right now" I said taking my helmet off and just crying

"Jordan we can do this okay we will get through this like we always do" Jay said trying to help

"Not this time because I know what I have to do if the time comes" I said crying more

"What do you have to do Jordan I don't understand" Jay said confused

"If he creates the Galactic Core it could end everything except his team, family, or friends. Same goes for us but whoever makes it explode will die instantly no matter what power you have or if you live forever" I said pulling myself together

"Jordan, are you saying you're going to be the one to sacrifice yourself to save everyone else" Jay said to me not knowing how to feel

"Yes, so all of you can live your lives and move forward it's not fair to you guys"

"Jordan, do you hear yourself right now...we all have something to lose if we die" Jay said to me pissed

"Jay, listen I couldn't let you do that okay...you are my best friend so is Hesh I'm never going to let yourself" I said to Jay upset

"Jordan, it won't come to that okay I know it won't"

"You really don't know that Jay"

"I do know that Jordan we got this"

"Jay, all I'm saying is If I comes to me having the core, I will be dying for you all...end of story" I said looking at Jay in his eyes

"Ugh okay...alright man" Jay said to me and then left my office

It was a very weird day that day just so many emotions all at once. I went to the top of The Tower and just looked out over the city I really needed it. I really felt terrible for making that decision but I didn't have a choice. Having someone else I care about die I couldn't let myself let them do that I just couldn't. It's up to me to find the remaining cores they are better in our hands than his.

"So, I heard what you have been saying about the cores and you" Scarlet said walking up to me "Yeah it was a matter of time in till you heard about it" I said to Scarlet

"Do you really think that's a good idea Jordan"

"No, it's a terrible idea but it needs to be made to save others"

"But it's you we are talking about Jordan; I need you so does your kids" Scarlet said tearing up

"I know but I can't have one of you guys do that it has to be me" I said starting to tear up

"There has to be another way Jordan" Scarlet said crying

"I don't know if there is we just have to wait and see Scarlet" I said wiping tears away

"Just don't die Jordan if you do it better be because it was your only option" Scarlet said pulling herself back together then leaving

Looking over the city sometimes makes the pain go away but not all the time...I wish It did but it doesn't. I had teams sent out to find the remaining cores so we have a chance of getting some before he could. We were able to retrieve the Dark Matter Core, All-knowing core, and the air core. Which means other me has the water core, Void core, and Gama Ray Burst core so he will definitely be here to get the others. We waited thinking he would show up in minutes since he wanted them so badly but he didn't. Maybe he didn't know Earth 2 existed or maybe it did but in a different part of the universe...we are talking about the multiverse here so anything is possible. I went home after being up on the roof of The Tower for three hours. When I got to the front door, I walked in to see Athena on the couch watching TV by herself.

"Daddy your home" She said running into my arms she squeezed me so hard I thought I was going to break a bone

"Yeah, I'm home and what are you doing out of bed little firebird" I said as I kneeled down and smiled

"Waiting for you to get home daddy I missed you" Athena said

"Well, I'm sure you wanted the part of the story as well huh" I said laughing a bit

"Well, that to but also so I don't have to worry about you" Athena said

“Kiddo that’s my job to worry about you...now how about I bring you ice cream up after I talk to your mother and after ice cream and story time” I said with some tears in my eyes

“Yayyy yes please...thank you daddy” Athena said then walked up stairs

I walked into the bedroom to see Scarlet sleeping on her right-side towards the window. When I saw her sleeping, I was taking my time trying not to wake her. My suit deactivating isn’t too loud but the dresser drawers are a bit squeaky. I put the circle to activate my suit on my night stand then went to get clothing from my dresser.

“Hey your home late” Scarlet said waking up from the squeak of the drawers

“Yeah, I am but I’m home now don’t need to worry” I said as I started to change

“Where were you at this whole time” Scarlet said a bit angry

“On the roof of The Tower so I can clear my head”

“Our daughter was worried”

“I know she was on the couch watching TV when I walked in... I just can’t believe Athena is a teenager and is already worrying about her father” I said as I teared up a bit

“She does worry a lot so do I Jordan we all worry actually...we all want you to live and not die being a hero” Scarlet said with tears in her eyes

“I changed the plan when I was up there so if everything goes to plan no one will be dying...I promise” I said to Scarlet

“What...you changed it to what” Scarlet said starting to smile

“Yes, but you will find out when the day comes baby...but I promise you I’ll be alive” I smiled at Scarlet and left to see Athena

I grabbed the ice cream for Athena and me. When I did, I walked up to her room and opened the door. “I got the ice the cream and the stories” I said laughing

“Yayyy what kind did you grab” Athena said as she started smiling

“Only the best ice cream in the world...Rocky Road ice cream” I said while giving Athena her bowl of ice cream

“You are right Rocky Road is the best ice cream” She said after eating some

“So do you remember where we left off” I said to Athena

“Umm you just went to a new world after giving people homes” Athena said

“Thats right so...we had to find a way to provide food for my people so I had to think of an idea quickly. So, after a while I found out there was a planet where dragons lived that planet also had food like meat, crops, and water. I built a portal to go there when I did it was beautiful. They lived in this gigantic tree it was taller than The Tower.

The adventure was just beginning for me but that's all for tonight my little firebird" I said smiling at her

"Wow how do you do so much like that in such short time" Athena said amazed

"I really don't know I just kinda winged it and it turned out great" I said to Athena

"Daddy, I want to be just like you when I grow up" "I'm sure you'll be the greatest Creator to be around it" I said with a big smile on my face

"Goodnight daddy I love you" Athena said

"Goodnight my little firebird...I love you to"

After that I went downstairs to the living room to watch TV for a bit. I turned on the TV to watch whatever was on so I could just relax but then the news said something about multiple ships entered the atmosphere. Then the feeling I had about the ships were true the ships started to fire on the city. After seeing this I ran into the bedroom to wake Scarlet up.

"Baby get the kids out of Earth 2 now" I said yelling a bit

"Where to and what's going on" Scarlet said confused

"He is here so I need you to take them to Chapel right now"

"Alright I will don't worry okay...just please be careful and you better be alive when we get back" Scarlet said to me hugging me

"I don't want to promise you anything but...I will try my best to stay alive for you and the kids" I said to Scarlet

"I love you baby" Scarlet said after she kissed me

"I love you to" I said back to Scarlet

I grabbed my suit activator and activated my suit. I went to The Tower to find Hesh and Jay so we could get prepared for the fight ahead. When I got into The Tower everyone was panicking and just so lost on what to do. I went to my office to find Hesh and Jay waiting for me.

"Dude he is here" Hesh said

"Yeah, I can see that" I said to Hesh a bit scared

"So, what's the plan Jordan...What are you going to do" Jay said to me a bit nervously

"We fight and we don't stop intill they are all gone you got me...no one dies today okay not even me" I said to them both

"Okay then let's kick some multiverse ass then" Hesh said to us

"Yeah, let's kick some ass guys" Jay said to us

“We got this...I believe in you both” I said to them

We all got prepared for another war which I kinda was over having to fight all the time. The army was also prepared for the battle ahead but we all met on the battle field.

“You have what I want Creator so just hand them over and no one has to die...I promise” The other me said to me

“No, I’m not going to give you a weapon that can destroy the universe Creator” I said to the other me

“Listen I’m not known as The Creator...I’m known as The Fracture” he said with a such hatred behind the words The Creator

“Well Fracture I’m not letting you take the cores...I’m not going to let you kill the universe that’s not how we are” I said trying to get through to him

“Well, I’m not you...I’m not as soft as you are Creator, I did a lot to get where I am now and I’m not going to let you stop me” Fracture said with such hatred

“Well then, you’re going to die Creator...along with every single one of your followers and your best friends”.

Fracture started to run towards us along with his army of weird looking people with all black outfits. Their helmets were broken glass put back together with fragments floating around their helmets. Fracture had my suit on but his helmet was cracked all over the place but some of the glass chunks were floating around his mask as well. Our two armies clashed my men were fighting back so well. His army was not doing the greatest to start off so we had the upper hand right now. Fracture tackled me to the ground after we both came to a stop, he jumped onto me and started to beat my helmet over and over. I waited for an opening so I could grab his arm to pop it out of place. I found the opening and was able to pop his arm out of place. I kicked him back and off of me. He got up but I kicked his knee back making him fall face first onto the ground. Fracture kicked my feet out from under me and got back on top of me. I held his head his head down so it would hurt his neck. He punched my ribs over and over intill I let go then he got off of me.

“Creator, you are not as soft as I thought you would be” Fracture said with an evil laugh

“Fracture, is this what you wanted to watch the world burn” I said out of breath

“Yes, watching the plan unfold is a beauty to me” Fracture said looking at the destruction

“Your just crazy Fracture that’s all you are...what happened to you to make you like this” I said to him

“Everything happened to me...my mother, father, uncle, and brother killed everyone I loved...they took everything away from me. They killed my family they killed my friends when I was at rock bottom that’s when I knew what I had to do. I Trained when I got good enough, I killed them all slowly like they did to my family. So, it took me down the dark path of being this person but I don’t ever want to stop doing this”.

After he said that he kicked dirt at me after he did that, he punched my helmet. I went back a few steps but I caught myself before I fell. I was able to upper cut him then elbow his chest. Then I jumped onto his neck and flipped him onto his back as I landed on my feet. I then kicked his helmet but when I did, he stabbed my other leg which made me fall down to my knees. He got ahold of my foot and started to crawl onto me. When he did, he knocked me out. Jay woke me up a couple of minutes later saying Fracture is trying to find the cores.

“Where is he now Jay” I said trying to get up

“He’s somewhere in The Tower looking for the cores” Jay said after helping me up

“I’m going after him Jay...keep fighting down here” I said to Jay out of breath

“Are you sure Jordan, I can help you” Jay said concerned

“I’m sure Jay like I said no one dies today” I said before walking into The Tower

After that I started to make my way up to my office. When I finally reached that floor Fracture had five guys patrolling the floor.

“So, who wants to go first” I said as I walked into the surveillance room

“Get him” The one guy yelled

I ran toward one kicking him through a wall. Then rolling onto the floor punching the one guys leg. I got up quickly two of them started to attack so I backed up a bit. The two in front of me and there was a guy behind me this was going to be fun. I waited intill one of them made a move and when one guy did finally make a move, I broke his left arm with my knee. Then ducked the attack from the guy behind me which made him hit the guy in front of me. I picked up a knife from the guy laying on the floor and threw it into the back of the guy who hit his partner. He fell to the ground as the other guy ran toward me, I ducked his attack. He swung his sword four times intill I was able to grab his hand to disarm him. When I disarmed him, I stabbed him with his sword right through the chest and out the other side.

“Now onto the big man” I said trying to take in as much air as possible

I walked into my office to see Fracture sitting in my office chair.

“Glad you could finally see me Jordan” Fracture said to me

“You’re not getting the cores Fracture” I said a bit pissed

“Listen I know where you put them, I also know that you’re the only one who can open the safe you put them in...so that means I can open it to” he said as he got up to walk around the room

“You won’t get them Fracture they were taken off world...you see I had time to think on the top of this place. Two decisions I had to make either I was going to die saving everyone or put the cores somewhere you’d never find them. So, I went with the second option that was hiding them on the ship my girlfriend and kids took to leave this planet” I said to Fracture with a very confident tone "you just killed your family Jordan" he said to with a very dark tone

I ran towards him and tackled him out the window as we were falling, I was punching his helmet over and over again. Fracture didn't hit the ground he started to fly somehow but after that I just passed out from the pain. Three hours went by and I finally woke up in the medical wing of The Tower. I felt in so much pain in my chest but I could also feel my healing kicking in as well.

"You took a worse beating this time man" Jay said sitting to my right

"Jay...it's you" I said with not much of a voice

"Save your words Jordan...Scarlet and your kids are safe they are at home right now. Fracture got away with none of the cores but I know he will be back" As Jay said this I kinda relaxed a bit in the bed

"Thank you" I said to Jay with the little breath I had left

"Your welcome man" Jay said tearing up

I passed out again but I know why I did this time. Knowing everything is alright and taken care of for now I could finally rest. When I woke up this time I was met with Scarlet and the kids.

"Hey guys you okay" I said feeling better than ever

"I think we should be asking you that baby" Scarlet said smiling

"Daddy you're okay right" Athena said happier than ever

"Yes, my little firebird I'm perfectly fine" I said to Athena but after I said that to her, I looked at Link

"Are you okay Link" I asked him

"Yeah, I'm fine dad" he said looking down

"Are you sure you're okay" I said asking again

"Yes, I'm fine dad" he said a bit angry

"Hey could me and Link talk privately please" I said to Scarlet

"Yeah of course" she said then left the room with Athena

"Now what's going on Link" I asked him

"Seeing you like that and having to do this dumb job"

"Hey Link the people out there can't protect themselves from everything out in the universe" I explained

"So why do you have to dad" he said crying

"Because if I don't then who will protect you, your mom, or your sister. People out there aren't like me

Link so it became my job to protect them and our family" I said as I sat him next to me

"But why can't you just stop doing this job dad"

"Because people look to me for all their answers, I protect a whole planet Link and someday maybe you'll do the same but for now I'm their God they believe in me to help them...just you rely on me to help you with homework or help you with problems at school" I tried to explain

"So, they see you as their parent" he said starting to understand

"Exactly they see me as their parent" I said to him

"I could do the same one day...like you dad" Link said

"If you wanted to yes, I'd train you like my sensei did" I said to Link

"What's a sensei"" Link said confused

"It's like a trainer to help you get better at something"

"You'd train me to be like you dad"

"Yes, if you wanted to, I would train you" I said to Link

"Then I would want to train dad" Link said so serious

"I will but now right now okay when your older" I told him

"Alright dad I understand"

"Now go take care of your mom and sister intill I get home okay"

"Yes, I will dad don't worry"

"Thank you Link".

Link hopped off the bed and went out to Scarlet and Athena. I'm so proud of my kids already they are so understanding and so worried about Scarlet and I it's just like me when I was a kid. Having kids really did change my life for the better having them made we stronger and more confident.

Chapter 8
The System

The project that I've been working on has finally been finished. It will bring more protection to Earth 2 more homes for other universal beings. It is called The System which yes, it's what it sounds like we been creating terraformed planets for anyone to live on. Earth 2 was the only planet in this Solar System but not anymore. We have added rocky terrestrial worlds, Gas giants, ice giants, Ocean planets, and Earth 2 like planets with some changes as well for other beings that can't breathe oxygen. So now we have 28 new planets in our Solar System we also already have homes built, Towers for communication, Food and water, and just everything else you can think of we have in The System.

"So, what did you guys think of the presentation I did on TV for its" I said to Hesh and Jay as I sat in my office chair

"Well, it was kinda cringy to see you doing those were movements with your hands" Hesh said and laughed

"Yeah, did they make you do that are something because if not why did you do the arm movements" Jay said before laughing as well

"Oh my god you guys...yes, they told me to do that so it would catch people's attention" I said giggling but trying to stay serious

"I mean the only thing I caught was a headache am I right" Hesh said before laughing uncontrollably along with Jay doing the same

"You guys are something else you know that...you really are" I said laughing in between the sentence

"Hey don't worry its good Jordan we had to make a bit of fun of it as you did with us on Earth 1 with like everything" Hesh said pulling himself together

"Okay fair enough" I said to Hesh

After all of that I went home to see everyone about to head to bed for the night.

"Hey kids before you go to bed you want to see something awesome" I said when I walked into the living room

"Well yeah daddy" Athena said excited

"Yes please" Link said excited as well

"Alright let's go then" I said to them and kissed Scarlet goodnight

We went to The Tower when we got there, we went to the portal room. I put the coordinates to Dragon Heart into the portal's computer.

"Where are we going daddy" Athena said curious

"Somewhere truly magical Athena it's actually a place I told you about in the stories" I said to Athena hoping she would figure it out

"Wait what stories" Link said

"Well see you didn't want to be tucked in at night but Athena did and she falls asleep with stories so I told her how I got to Earth 2" I told Link

"Oh, I thought you were born here dad...on Earth" Link said confused

"I was born on Earth 1 where everything was different but Earth 1 was consumed in lava and just molten rock so I took people to my creation called Earth 2 which is here...I saved a lot of lives but I couldn't save everyone sadly" I said to Link

After that the portal opened in front of us so I held their hands and we all walked through together. We were met with the pretty night sky of Dragon Heart. The moons glow of a soft blue and white were shinning on everything.

"This is Dragon Heart guys where we got our food from for the longest time" I said to them both

"This is Dragon Heart daddy" Athena said to me so amazed

"Yes, it is Athena" I said back to her

"Dad how did you find this place" Link said also amazed

"Your mom gave me the coordinates for this place but she had no idea it was a dragon filled planet" I said to Link

"But I want you guys to meet someone that helped me hes pretty cool. Also, hes the leader of these lands so be careful of what you do" I explained to them

We all walked to the great tree which we saw when we got there. Just the walk is a bit of a pain but it's worth it of course. We finally arrived at the tree but two hours passed so we really had a nice walk. I helped them climb the tree up to the very top of the tree that's where Scar normally is.

“Hey Scar long time no see” I said to Scar

“Creator, indeed it has been a long time” Scar said back to me

“How have things been I know they were rough but hopefully better” I said to Scar

“Yeah, way better now...Who are those two hiding behind you” Scar said trying not to Scare them

“These are my kids...Athena is my daughter and Link is my son” I explained to Scar

“Well, it’s very nice to meet the both of you so very nice to meet you. I have a surprise for you though Creator” Scare said then moved his gigantic tail to revel an egg

“Wow so we both ended up having kids then” I said laughing a bit

“Indeed, we did...the wife convinced me somehow” Scar chuckled after saying that

“Yep, so did my girlfriend so I get it but now I feel like a true protector and more of a real creator” I explained to him

“I get the feeling I really do...I just can’t wait to teach him how to fly and help me watch over my paradise you know” Scar said sounding very happy

“I really do understand that feeling Scar I really do” I said to him

We stayed there for a while talking and the kids started to talk to Scar after a while. We talked about how I was there asking for help and all that stuff in the very beginning. After about 4 more hours of talking, we all went back home since the kids were tired and I had to make sure Earth 2 was still safe from Fracture. When we got home, I carried both of them to their beds and tucked them in. I got into our room placing my activator on my night stand. I looked out the big window really hoping Fracture would just go back to his universe. Thinking about anyone getting hurt just really makes me sick you know I’m tired of fighting wars and one day I may die during one of them. Maybe Hesh or Jay my family who knows what lies ahead of me and the future of Earth 2. I’m just going to try my damn best to protect the people I love and so should you. Be the change you wanna see be the hero in your own story because there’s a lot of people who pick the dark side. It’s up to us to defeat them together on this journey. I’m The Creator and this is me signing of once again but the adventure is only just beginning for you and I whoever is reading this. Whoever is reading this I hope to see you on my creation... Earth 2.

THE END